For Tim, the funny one, with love
J. P. L.

For Daniel and Molly
S. B.

Text copyright © 2006 by J. Patrick Lewis
Illustrations copyright © 2006 by Simon Bartram

The poem "Schoolteacher" previously appeared in
Light Quarterly; Reader's Digest; and *The Bedford Introduction to Literature,* 4th ed.,
Michael Meyer, ed., St. Martin's Press, Bedford Books, 1996.

First edition 2006

Library of Congress Cataloging-in-Publication Data is available.

Library of Congress Catalog Card Number 2005054217

ISBN-10 0-7636-1837-3
ISBN-13 978-0-7636-1837-7

2 4 6 8 10 9 7 5 3

Printed in China

This book was typeset in Truesdell.
The illustrations were done in acrylic.

Candlewick Press
2067 Massachusetts Avenue
Cambridge, Massachusetts 02140

visit us at www.candlewick.com

Once Upon a Tomb

GRAVELY HUMOROUS VERSES

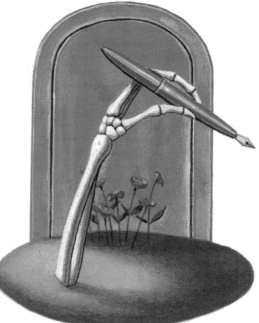

J. Patrick Lewis

illustrated by Simon Bartram

CANDLEWICK PRESS
CAMBRIDGE, MASSACHUSETTS

DAIRY FARMER

. . .

Here lies little Larry LeGow,

Who sat in the shade

Of his Hereford cow,

Tied up her tail

Behind a hind udder,

Filled a milk bucket

For Saturday's butter.

Flew off the stool,

Went down on his knees,

Coaxing his cow

For some Sunday cream cheese.

Here is a lesson

for Larry LeGow:

NEVER SIT UNDER

A HEREFORD COW.

UNDERWEAR SALESMAN

• • •

Our grief

Was brief.

FOOD CRITIC

. . .

Spinach gags you.
Gravy spills.
Beets are poison.
Liver kills.
Lima beans are
Worse than peas.
Bury me with
Pizza, please.

School Principal

• • •

He taped this elementary rule
To all the restroom stalls at school.
Here's a lesson to re-*pee*-t:

PLEASE PUT DOWN
THE TOILET SEAT!

FISHERMAN

• • •

Here lies Henry
"Hook 'Em" Hawes,
Who went overboard
Because
Lobsters exercised
His jaws.
Ate the lobsters . . .
And the claws!

POET

· · ·

Reader, if I had more time
I'd say *au revoir* in rhyme,
Sayonara, ciao in verse—
But I have to catch a hearse.

FORTUNE TELLER

• • •

Here lies.

TATTOO ARTIST

• • •

No clothes,

No shoes

Inside his

Box of pine,

Only a body

Tattoo—

By design.

SCHOOLTEACHER

...

Knives can harm you, heaven forbid!

Axes may disarm you, kid.

Guillotines are painful, but . . .

There's nothing like a paper cut.

Lighthouse Keeper

...

He swept a beam across the bay
That set the barges on their way.
A dozen lights shone past the pier—
The coast had never been so clear.
Though now his lamp is ever dim,
Twelve captains will remember him.

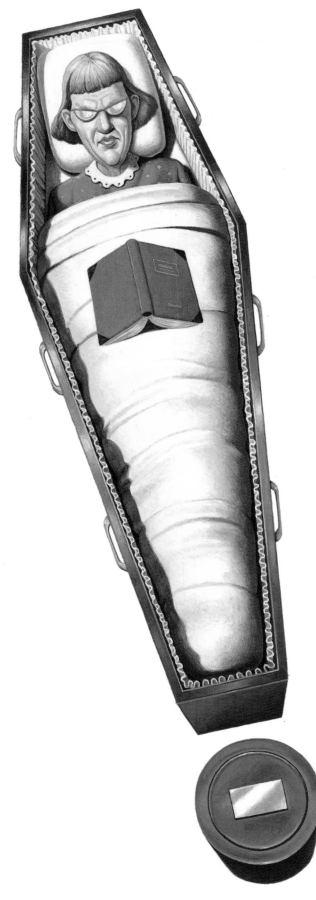

BOOK EDITOR

...

Miss Spelling's
Exclamation points
Were myriad!!!
She lived on
The margin.
And died.
Period.

GARDENER

• • •

When his days concluded,

His final wish was granted:

First he was uprooted.

Then he was transplanted.

MAILMAN

• • •

Returned to Sender.

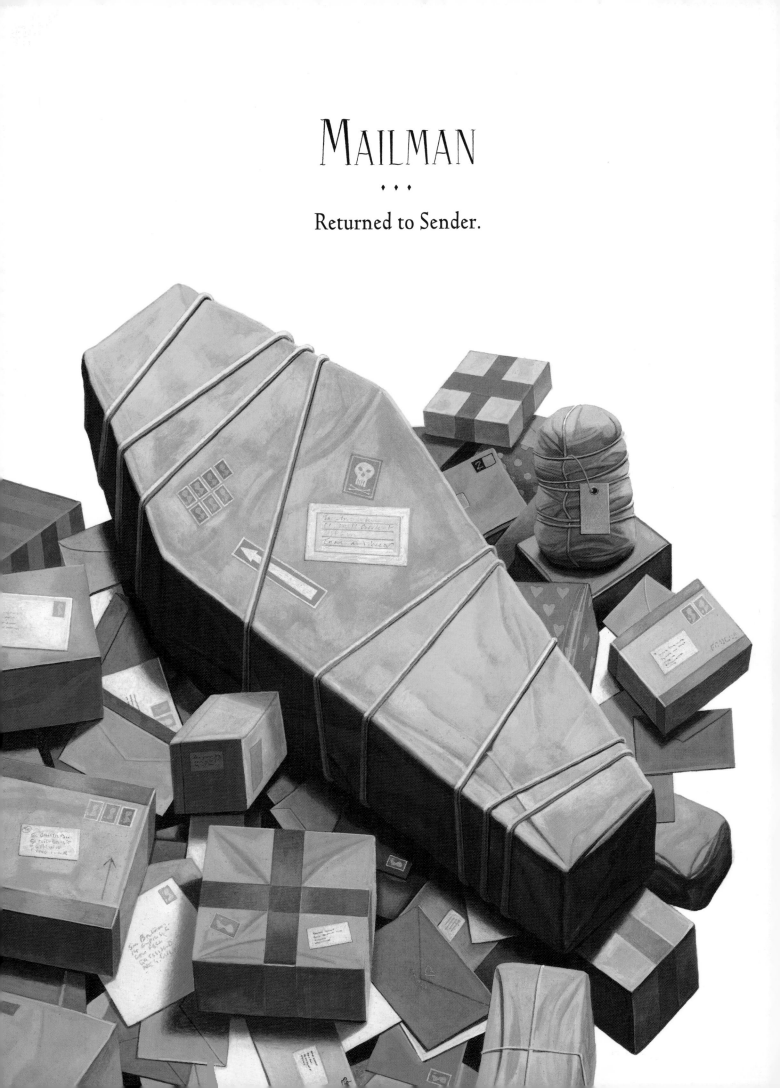

MOVIE STAR

• • •

Movie actress Holly Gooden,
Duller than vanilla puddin',
Tried to act but simply couldn't.
Holly would but Hollywoodn't.

GRAVEDIGGER

• • •

It is a blessing that he died.

Bless his shovel, bless his soul.

Can you imagine if he'd lived?

He'd have to dig himself a hole.

BULLY

. . .

Once he wasted guys
Like flies.
Now he comes to terms
With worms.

SOCCER PLAYER

• • •

Ball thumped Albert on the head—
Looked like a tractor-tire tread.

Ball whacked Albert on the snout—
Looked like one big Brussels sprout.

Ball boxed Albert on the ears—
Looked like smoke alarms from Sears.

Ball socked Albert on the jaw—
Looks like Albert's last hurrah.

WEIGHTLIFTER

* * *

Unh . . .

Unh . . .

Unh . . .

Uh-uh.

KNOW-IT-ALL

· · ·

There's nothing
Roger didn't know.
(Except that red
Does not mean Go!)

CAFETERIA LADY

· · ·

Here lie the bones of Mabel Grady,
Extremely thoughtful school-lunch lady.

She never served a Jell-O mold
If it was more than six weeks old.

BEAUTICIAN

. . .

Honey loved to beehive hair—
Could have been a millionaire
Turning that gold swivel chair.

Made a fortune on chloride
Bleach. But after she blow-dried,
Honey flipped, curled up, 'n' dyed.